(now go to bed)

by jonnyHal

layout inspired by Chris Cava Preston

for Loren and Bo,
there'd be no story without you.
-jHal

ISBN 978-0692687161
Library of Congress Control Number: 2016905756

Printed in the U.S.A.

First CreateSpace printing, June 2016

Book design by JonnyHal.
Illustrations by Shutterstock.
The text for this book is set in Adobe Caslon Pro.

original  *production*

jLoBo_Press

Looking for a great bedtime story?

Sorry.
Some other kid must have gotten the last one.
Too bad, so sad.

Just kidding.
Every book* must have a story, right?

*movies on the other hand...

How about we set sail
on an epic pirate adventure...

Learn fancy words like

dis-com-bob-u-late

adjective: to confuse and befuddle

And bid farewell to interplanetary objects?

"Goodnight Asteriod X8742!"

Too bad there's no story
like <u>that</u> in here.

Besides, it's not like you'd be interested
in a slightly used fairy tale*

*told only on special occasions

About a beautiful
(but poor) princess....

Who finds a magical unicorn named Sparkle...

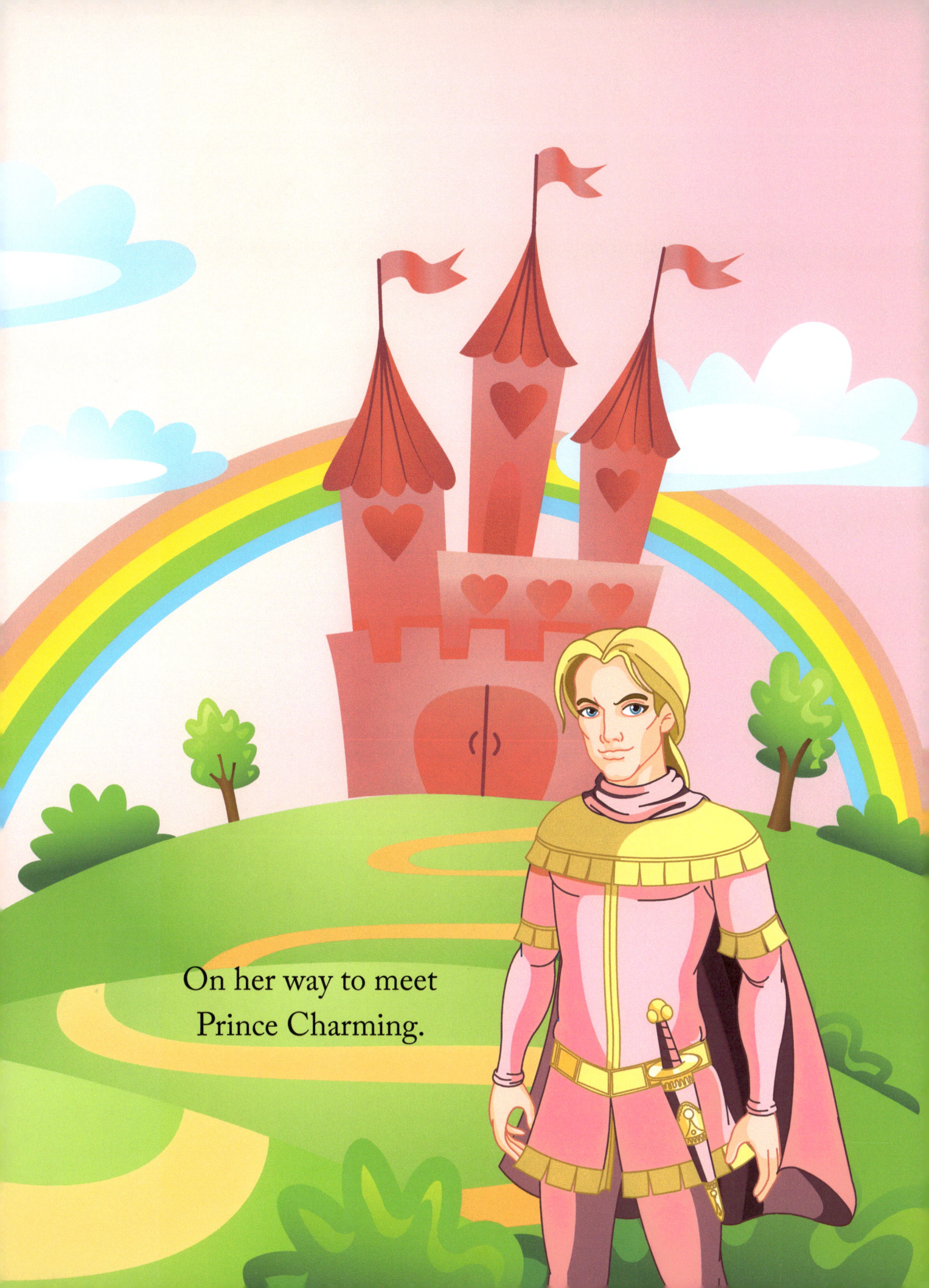

On her way to meet
Prince Charming.

Which is a good thing because
that story actually gets a bit weird.

Turns out the Princess *really* liked to shop*...

*which explains her whole poor thing

The Prince wasn't exactly charming...

And Sparkle had a few issues of his own.

FUN FACT
Parents should spend at least

minutes reading to their kids every night.

How long have we been reading*?

*there's still time for one very VERY short story

The kind of story that begins with a big kiss...

Followed by some magic words.

Say them with me:
Goodnight
I Love You
Now and forever
Or at least until
Pickles turn purple...

DO NOT EAT
any pickle that is purple*.

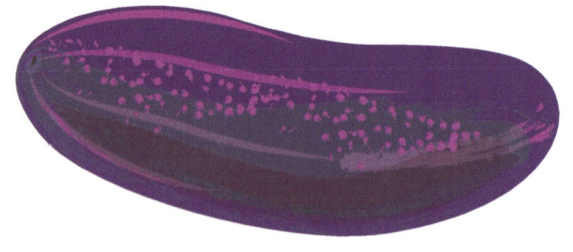

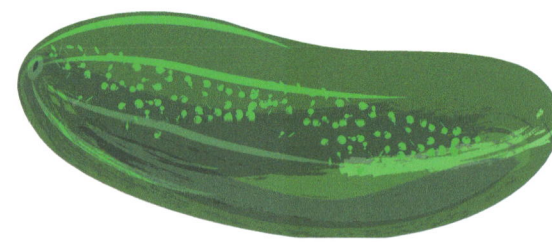

NO

YES

*if you did, don't worry - it's probably just an eggplant

Yes, a chicken is also an "egg plant".

But that's a whole other story.
Now it's time to close your eyes
because we're all out of words

and there's nothing left to see.

Except for this crazy koo-koo land.

(now go to bed)

about the author

When not still staring thoughtfully into the distance, Jonny Hal is an award-winning TV writer, editor, and producer. Jonny lives in Pacific Palisades, California with his awesome wife, terrific son, and 2 crazy dogs -- a situation that ensures a never-ending supply of love, encouragement, and rich source material for future stories.

other titles by jonnyHal

THIS BOOK IS OVER! (now go to sleep)

www.ingramcontent.com/pod-product-compliance
Lightning Source LLC
Chambersburg PA
CBHW041605120626
46551CB00002B/320